THE HIDDEN MESSAGE

Written by
DAVID BOYD

Illustrated by
JEFF ALWARD

WILLIAM SHAKESPEARE

KIT MARLOWE

RICHARD BURBAGE

FRANCIS WALSINGHAM

ELIZABETH I

REAL PEOPLE IN HISTORY

WILLIAM (WILL) SHAKESPEARE (1564–1616) was the greatest English writer and poet of all time.

CHRISTOPHER (KIT) MARLOWE (1564–1593) was a well-known poet and playwright.

RICHARD BURBAGE (1567–1619) was a famous Elizabethan actor. His father, James Burbage, was a friend of Shakespeare's.

FRANCIS WALSINGHAM (1530–1590) was head of the Queen's spy network.

ELIZABETH I (1533–1603) was Queen of England.

FICTIONAL CHARACTER

JASPER KYD is a child actor in this story.

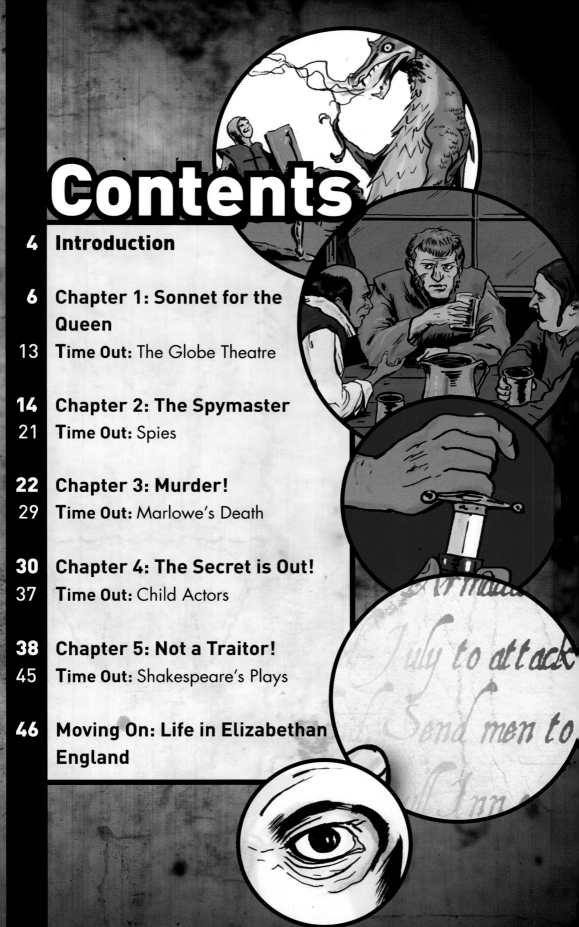

Contents

This story takes place in the reign of Queen Elizabeth I. She was Queen of England from 1558–1603. Her long reign is known as the Elizabethan Age.

1533 »	1558 »	1564 »	1571 »	1586 »
Elizabeth is born at Greenwich Palace.	Elizabeth becomes Queen of England.	William Shakespeare and Christopher Marlowe are born in the same year.	Elizabeth names Francis Walsingham chief spymaster.	The supporters of Mary, Queen of Scots plan to remove Elizabeth from the throne.

ENGLAND

This was a remarkable time in the history of England. England was a rich and powerful country. English explorers sailed to many places to discover new lands.

London was the center of art and literature. Shakespeare and other playwrights wrote some of the best works of English poetry and literature during this period. Plays were very popular, and the theater was a favorite form of entertainment.

Queen Elizabeth had spies to protect her from her enemies. She died at the age of 70.

William Shakespeare

WHAT'S THE STORY? This story is set in an actual time in history and depicts real people, but some of the characters and events are fictitious.

1587 »	1588 »	1593 »	1603 »	1616 »
Mary, Queen of Scots is put to death.	Philip II of Spain attacks England and is defeated.	Christopher Marlowe dies.	Queen Elizabeth I dies. James I becomes King of England.	William Shakespeare dies.

THE GLOBE THEATRE

The new Globe Theatre

The Globe Theatre was built in 1598. It stood on the bank of the Thames River in London. Many of Shakespeare's plays were performed in this theater.

The Globe Theatre was octagonal (eight-sided) in shape and opened to the sky in the center. It could seat up to 3,000 people.

The stage was roughly a quarter of the size of a basketball court. It had trapdoors in its floor and ropes overhead for stage work. There was no way to light the stage at night, so plays were performed only in the afternoon.

The Globe Theatre burned down in 1613 when a cannon set the roof on fire. The theater was rebuilt almost immediately. It was torn down in 1644 to make room for houses.

In 1997, a new Globe Theatre was built near the site of the old one. The building and the stage were designed to be as close to the original as possible. In its first year, the new Globe drew an audience of nearly a quarter of a million people.

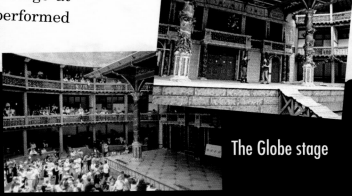

The Globe stage

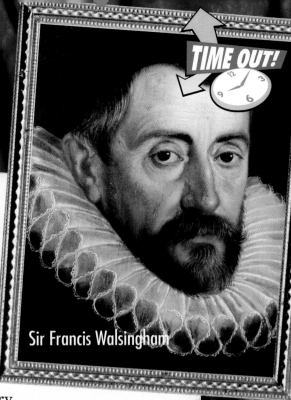

TIME OUT!

Sir Francis Walsingham

Queen Elizabeth I had many enemies. She was a Protestant queen. Many Catholics in England wanted her dead so they could have a Catholic on the throne.

The Queen became an enemy of Spain when she refused to marry Philip II of Spain. He decided to send warships to attack England.

The Queen was afraid for her life. She had a network of spies to protect her. Sir Francis Walsingham was her spymaster. Christopher (Kit) Marlowe is believed to have been another of the Queen's spies.

Spies reported things they saw and conversations they overheard. They also secretly read other people's letters.

Spies used vinegar, sour milk, or lemon juice to write secret messages. These secret messages could be read when the paper was carefully heated over a candle flame.

July to attack

Send men to

MARLOWE'S DEATH

TIME OUT!

Christopher Marlowe was a friend of Shakespeare's and a talented writer. Like Shakespeare, he wrote many plays for the theater.

Marlowe died when he was only 29. Who killed him? Why? There are many questions around the death of Marlowe. Records that might tell us more either never existed or were destroyed over the years. His death remains a mystery today.

BACK AT SHAKESPEARE'S ...

WILL, WE HAVE TERRIBLE NEWS.

WHAT IS IT?

KIT MARLOWE HAS BEEN STABBED TO DEATH!

THE NEWS SHOCKS SHAKESPEARE.

KIT? WHY? HOW?

AN ARGUMENT OVER THE BILL. HE WAS STABBED AND BLED TO DEATH.

KIT WAS IN THIS VERY ROOM THIS MORNING! HE TOOK ONE OF MY SONNETS. I WISH I COULD TELL HIM NOW THAT I DIDN'T MIND.

... AND THEN YOU SAW THAT I HAD WRITTEN A FRESH COPY OF THE SONNET. THE ORIGINAL WAS NO LONGER NEEDED.

YES. BUT MR. BURBAGE AND RICHARD SAW ME. PLEASE LET ME PLAY MERCUTIO! PLEASE DON'T TAKE THAT AWAY FROM ME!

WILL, DO WHAT YOU WANT WITH JASPER. FIRE HIM IF YOU WISH. I WON'T OBJECT.

I'VE BEEN CALLED TO DEPTFORD TO IDENTIFY POOR MARLOWE'S BODY AND TO TAKE CARE OF HIS BURIAL.

WE'LL ALL MEET TOMORROW NIGHT TO REMEMBER HIM.

WE WILL INDEED!

An Elizabethan acting company

CHILD ACTORS

In Shakespeare's theater, there were 26 actors. Ten of them were boys. The rest were men. There were no female actors.

People did not approve of female actors, so women's roles were played by boys. Child actors regularly performed in theaters in Elizabethan England.

A strict religious group called the Puritans was strongly opposed to the theater. In 1642, they forced theaters to close for over 10 years. By the time the theaters reopened, there were no boys trained for the stage. So women took on the female roles. However, it was many years before people approved of female actors.

NOW WE WILL DRINK IN MEMORY OF OUR FRIEND.

I DELIVERED EVERYTHING TO THE BANK ON LONDON BRIDGE. IS IT ALL RIGHT IF I JOIN THE OTHERS?

JASPER HAS NO IDEA HOW MUCH HARM HE HAS CAUSED.

AS FOR ME, WHAT DO I KNOW? I KNOW THAT KIT MARLOWE WAS NO TRAITOR TO HIS QUEEN!

I OWE KIT MARLOWE ONE LAST FAVOR. AND I KNOW WHERE I'LL FIND IT ...

TWO HOURS LATER, IN WALSINGHAM'S ROOM.

MASTER SHAKESPEARE, HER MAJESTY WAS VERY PLEASED WITH THE SONNET YOU SENT HER YESTERDAY.

SHAKESPEARE'S PLAYS

MR. WILLIAM
SHAKESPEARES
COMEDIES,
HISTORIES, &
TRAGEDIES.
Published according to the True Originall Copies.

LONDON
Printed by Isaac Iaggard, and Ed. Blount. 1623.

Shakespeare's plays are among the best ever written. In all, there are 37 plays that bear his name. Some examples are *Romeo and Juliet*, *Julius Caesar*, and *Hamlet*.

Only a few of Shakespeare's plays were published during his lifetime. Most were not printed until after his death. In 1623, several of Shakespeare's close friends collected all his plays and published them.

Shakespeare also wrote 154 sonnets. Many were beautiful love poems that people still read today.

MOVING ON

LIFE IN ELIZABETHAN ENGLAND

There was no Internet, television, or video games, so what did people do for entertainment? You'll be surprised!

English people during the Elizabethan Age worked hard, but they also played hard. Music was a big part of their lives. Wealthy families hired musicians to play music during their meals. The poor sang at work or enjoyed free public concerts. The fiddle, bagpipe, flute, and recorder were popular musical instruments.

Dancing was a popular pastime. And everyone enjoyed the theater. Puppeteers and acrobats were also popular.

Elizabethan men and women spent a lot of time on their hair. Men wore their hair shoulder length or put on wigs to look fashionable. Women dyed their hair and wore hair nets, jewels, pins, and hair combs.

Elizabethan fashion was influenced by the Spanish and French styles. Women wore tight-fitting gowns with big ruffle collars. Men wore silk stockings and leather shoes with cloaks and wide hats.

We are all familiar with Elizabethan fashion and costumes because Shakespeare's plays are still very popular today. And movies of Shakespeare's plays are box-office hits!

From the movie
Shakespeare in Love

INDEX